I0623181

HOLLY'S NOEL

ELLE E. KAY

FAITH WRITES PUBLISHING

Benton, Pennsylvania

Editor: Geesey Editorial Services

FAITH WRITES PUBLISHING

PO BOX 494, Benton
Pennsylvania 17814-0494

eBook ISBN: 978-0-9994856-6-8
Paperback ISBN: 978-1-950240-26-5

Books by Elle E. Kay

Faith Writes Publishing

Endless Mountain Series
Shadowing Stella
Implicating Claudia
Chasing Sofie

The Lawkeepers Contemporary Romance Series
Lawfully Held
A K-9 Lawkeeper Romance
Lawfully Defended
A SWAT Lawkeeper Romance
Lawfully Guarded
A Billionaire Bodyguard Lawkeeper Romance

The Lawkeepers Historical Romance Series
Lawfully Taken
A Bounty Hunter Lawkeeper Romance
Lawfully Given
A Christmas Lawkeeper Romance
Lawfully Promised
A Texas Ranger Lawkeeper Romance
Lawfully Vindicated
A US Marshal Lawkeeper Romance

Elle E. Kay

Blushing Brides Series
The Billionaire's Reluctant Bride
The Bodyguard's Fake Bride

Heroes of Freedom Ridge Series
Healing the Hero
A CHRISTIAN ARMY RANGER CHRISTMAS ROMANCE
Persuaded by the Hero
A CHRISTIAN ARMY RANGER CHRISTMAS ROMANCE
(Releases December 2021)

Standalone Novella
Holly's Noel

Chapter 1

Holly Ewing sat at her desk in the corner of her dining room. Words crawled slowly off the keyboard as she typed a "house for rent" ad to be run in the local paper. She would have to vet possible tenants. Spending days fielding phone calls wasn't an option, so she put her email address in as the contact. The best she could hope for was a quiet young lady. Of course, she couldn't put that in the advertisement. It would be considered discriminatory. Wouldn't it? She wasn't sure, but it was best to be cautious. Easy enough to pick a woman from the potential candidates by looking at her name.

In the meantime, she'd dust and vacuum and see if anything else needed to be done next door. She hurried in the back entrance of the home where she'd grown up. She cleared some cobwebs from the doorway before pulling cleaning supplies from the pantry. Soon she'd have this space shining like a sunbeam. It was her mother's expression. She'd always thought it odd, since sunbeams showed off the dust, but it was comforting now.

She went room by room, cleaning and collecting items to bring home with her. When she reached the living room, her eyes went to her granddaddy's shotgun hanging over the fireplace. There was a step ladder in the pantry. She got it, climbed up, and took the gun off the wall. The dust was thick, so she ran her rag over it. It could be cleaned better later on, after she got it home. It wasn't safe to leave it with a renter coming. If she remembered correctly, there was an ammunition box in the closet. She dug that up and added it to her pile of things to take home. Then she got back to cleaning.

Several hours later, the two-bedroom colonial was spotless. She rubbed her sore hands together as she stood looking out the front window at Lake Bethel. She stretched, trying to loosen the kinks in her neck. It was a gorgeous autumn day, the chill in the air was bitter, but from inside the gleam of the sun off the lake made it seem like summertime. Well, it would if it weren't for the bright reds and yellows of the leaves that blanketed the ground.

Glancing down at her fitness band, she noticed the time. It was getting late, and she needed to get started on an order of cupcakes. It was hard to keep herself from devouring the pumpkin ones with the cream cheese icing. She was making those and some caramel apple cupcakes for the fall festival committee meeting. She had a feeling they'd ordered these as a taste test and would order a larger batch for next week's festival. It would be a challenge to make enough, but she was up for it. She headed toward the back door and grabbed her coat from the hook.

Holly rushed out to deliver the cupcakes in

time for the six o'clock committee meeting. Norma Jean arrived at the same time and pulled open the heavy door, holding it until she made her way inside.

"Oh, Holly, they look delicious. I can't wait to try one. Maybe more than one."

"I hope you enjoy them."

"Thank you. Thank you. Thank you. I'm so excited to devour these."

It was the truth; Norma Jean was one of Holly's best customers. As many cupcakes as she ate, you would expect her to be overweight, but she barely had one hundred pounds on her 5'2" stature. "I'm glad you're excited. I'll set these down on the conference table and be on my way."

"You can't leave. We voted you onto the committee to take your mother's place. You do want to continue her legacy, don't you?"

Holly didn't sigh out loud. That would've been rude, but she wanted to. Her mother's legacy didn't depend on an annual festival. Wasn't she her mother's legacy? Wasn't it already secure? Margie Ewing had done so much for this community. Holly didn't say any of it. Instead, she asked, "When did you vote me onto the committee?"

"Last week. Didn't the secretary call you? Oh, that's right, you are the secretary. That was your mother's position."

So much for having time to bake enough cupcakes for the festival. That wasn't likely to happen if she was stuck being committee secretary. "Okay. I'll stay and see about this."

"Goodie, goodie, goodie. That is such great news." Norma Jean reached out a wrinkled hand and took one of each flavor cupcake. She made her way to a seat facing the row of windows. Patting the space next to her, she motioned that Holly should sit with her. Holly sat down in the seat indicated and crossed her legs. Her hip was bothering her, but she adjusted her position and ignored the pain. She glanced over as Norma Jean licked caramel filling off the back of her hand. How had she managed to get it there? She didn't chuckle out loud, but the urge was definitely there. She'd always liked her mother's friend, but Norma Jean was over-the-top.

Holly stacked the cookies she'd taken from the oven onto a decorative plate. She'd found the perfect fit for the rental as soon as the paper ran the ad. The woman found the rental on the internet. Holly sent her the lease, and she'd signed it and had it notarized. Everything was good to go. She was locked in for three months. Three glorious months that the house wouldn't sit empty and would actually bring Holly some much needed income. Baking was not a lucrative business in a small town.

Noel was a writer who was looking for a quiet retreat from the world where she could concentrate, so she'd be able to meet her deadlines. The arrangement couldn't be more perfect. Holly finished up the dishes from her baking, wiped them dry and stacked them back in the cabinet. Noel would arrive any moment and the smell of fresh baked cookies would greet her.

The doorbell rang. Holly hurried to the door

to meet her tenant.

"May I help you?" she asked the scruffy-looking man staring down at her. He moved closer filling the doorway. Spicy cologne assaulted her senses, so she took a step back.

"I'm Noel. Are you Holly?" He scratched at day-old stubble.

"Wait. What? You can't be. I was expecting Noel, like Christmas, not a null, like null and void."

"No. It's not like 'null,' Noel rhymes with coal, but it is spelled n-o-e-l."

"Null fits better since the lease will be null and void. I thought I was renting the house to a woman. I'm not prepared to have a man living that close to me when there are no neighbors for acres on either side."

"I have an iron clad lease here. You're not getting out of it that easy. Just show me in. Then we can get out of each other's hair. I'm here to work, not to flirt with the flour-dusted landlady."

Holly's hands betrayed her. She tried wiping

the flour from her jeans. She forced herself to stop. "Fine, come in, but I'll be taking the paperwork to my lawyer. I'll get out of the lease." She was so mad she wanted to slam the door and stomp, but she controlled herself. "Help yourself to the cookies. I baked them for the woman I thought was leasing the place."

"Thanks. They smell delicious." He smirked.

She gave him a quick tour and turned to leave.

"You're a fiery little thing, aren't you?"

"What did you ask me?"

"It wasn't meant to offend. It means you have spunk."

"Whatever. I have work to do."

"I'll be right here if you want to fight some more."

"We were not fighting."

"Sure, felt like we were."

"Whatever. I have to go."

"Fine. See you later?"

"I hope not too soon."

"Already decided you don't like me, huh?"

Ignoring that last question, she ducked out the back door and hurried into her kitchen entrance. How could she have missed something so huge? That primitive man with the tortoise shell eyes and sandy-blond hair could not stay in the house next door. He wasn't her perfect tenant. She grabbed the cordless phone to call her lawyer. He could see her the next morning. "Great. I'll take it. You won't believe what I've gotten myself into."

Noel Ryan chuckled to himself as he unpacked. His high-strung new landlady with the mahogany eyes would provide more inspiration than the beautiful setting ever could. The heroine in his book was a state trooper rather than a baker, but he could certainly add some of Holly's spunky personality to the character sketch. He could hardly wait to start writing. He stuffed his socks into the top drawer before giving up unpacking. He had to get words onto the screen.

Grabbing his laptop and cord, he set himself up in the living room to write. Maybe he'd light a fire later. Inspiration struck and couldn't be ignored. It was hours later when he took a break. He'd written three thousand words. Not bad at all. *Thank you, Miss Holly.* He inhaled deeply enjoying the scent of lilacs that lingered in the air from the feisty brunette. Now he had to figure out how to spend more time around the little sprite. He'd have his writing done in no time if she kept providing fodder.

For now, he needed food. It was time to check out the town.

He drove his silver Mercedes down Main Street. Not much happening. There were a couple of restaurants, nothing fancy. Pizza would do. He pulled into the parking lot. A teenage girl manned the hostess booth. She led him to a table overlooking the lake. Setting a menu in front of him, she said, "Candy will be right with you."

Candy was his waitress. A bleach blonde in an outfit two sizes too small. She touched his hand and smiled. Her flirtations came across loud and clear, but he wasn't interested.

Thoughts of his fiery landlady filled his head as he turned to stare out the window. The sunset was perfect, painted by the hand of God. It would be great to be in a boat right about now, if it weren't for the chill in the air.

Noel opened his notebook and began working on character sketches. Before long, Candy placed a large pizza on the table. Ignoring the food, he continued working. An hour later, he had barely touched the pizza, so he had it boxed up. He wondered where his appetite had gone. It wasn't like him to pick at his food. Of course, the pizza tasted like cardboard and the flour on the bottom was so thick it left his fingers white, so maybe it was the quality of the food that killed his appetite. He'd need to find a better place to eat. Or learn to cook, which wasn't likely to happen. Candy sashayed back up to the table and placed his check in front of him. She ripped a piece off another check and with a suggestive smile, jotted something down before tossing it on the table. He peered down at the paper. Candy was an attractive woman. It might even be fun to take her out, but he didn't plan to call her number. Noel paid for his meal and slipped the paper into his pocket along with his credit card. He'd left cash on the table for the tip. When he ducked back into his car, he emptied his pockets into the console. Glancing at the phone number, he considered crumpling it up, but didn't.

When he arrived back at the house, he started a fire. His laptop sat on the table, but it pulled him to it, like a siren's call. He reached for the computer. At the rate he was going, the story would write itself, and he could be home for Christmas.

There had to be a way out of this lease. That man didn't even tell her who he was. The temperature felt ten degrees colder in the building. Didn't Clive believe in heat? The high ceilings in the foyer probably didn't help keep the heat in. His office door was open, and she marched in prepared for battle.

He came out from behind a filing cabinet into

the cluttered room piled high with boxes of files. The beautiful old home had been converted to law offices, but you could barely appreciate the architecture with so much stuff crammed into the room.

Clive held out his hand to shake hers. "So, what brings you to my frozen tundra this morning, sweetie?" He moved some files off a chair, so she could sit. He took the chair behind his desk and rolled it closer to her.

"Why is this place so cold?" she asked.

"Heater went out. The chill off Lake Bethel makes it feel like January instead of September. Too bad I don't have a lovely fireplace to sit beside." His gaze went to the gorgeous fireplace with boxes of files stacked around it.

"Why don't you use the fireplace?"

"It probably hasn't been cleaned since before Dad took over the practice, so I don't think it's a good idea to light it without having someone out here to check it first. Enough small talk. What brings you in? You said something about trouble?"

"I signed on a tenant to live in Mom's place. Problem is, I thought I was renting it to a woman, but it turned out to be a man. I don't want the scoundrel there. He led me to believe he was a she."

"Does he sound like a woman? You did interview him and do a credit check, didn't you?"

"Well, no. It was all done by email correspondence. Noel. A beautiful womanly name. She sounded perfect, but then this unshaven hulk of a man walks up to my door. I was not looking for a male neighbor. I don't need the hassle."

"Do you have a lease?"

"Yes. I need to get out of it." She pulled it from her leather bag and handed it to him.

He closely inspected the document before handing it back. "You're not getting out of this. Everything is legal and binding. Where did you get the forms anyway? Why didn't you come to me?" He raised an eyebrow.

"I didn't want to bother you with something so petty, since you refuse to bill me more than half the time. So, I printed the paperwork from a legal website."

"Good job. Looks quite professional. I'm afraid there isn't much I can do here. Maybe you should consider the benefits of having a big strong man around? He can carry heavy grocery bags and take the garbage cans to the end of the drive. There are so many other manly tasks he could help with, if you would be nice to him." There was a sparkle in his eye. She resisted the temptation to let him bait her.

"So, I'm stuck with this man in the house next door until after Christmas?"

"I'm afraid so. Unless he does something to break his contractual obligations. You know, like not paying rent. But don't get me started on how long it can take to evict a tenant for non-payment. Just learn to get along with the man. It won't kill you, sweetie." He stood.

"Clive, don't call me sweetie. I haven't been your sweetie since fifth grade." She got up and walked toward the door.

"We could change that if you'd like?"

"I don't think so. You seem to prefer the bachelor lifestyle. Toby seems to fill your need for family. Not that I blame you, dogs make much better companions than people. Besides, I plan to stay a widow for the rest of my life. I already met and married my perfect man. Nobody could measure up to Kevin."

He feigned pulling an arrow from his heart as he took a step back. "Ouch." He approached her and gave her a one-armed hug. "Don't give up on your future."

"I haven't given up. My life is full. Business is booming. And I'm on the fall festival committee."

"How did you get suckered into that? Never mind. I have another client coming in. I'll walk you to your car."

Chapter 2

She carried two large trays laden with cup-cakes while attempting to weave her way through the crowd to the baked sale booth. The festival was already packed with people, and it was only ten in the morning. She lost her footing on the uneven grass and the tray started to slip from her hands, but before the cupcakes hit the ground, a strong arm grabbed her tray to hold it upright. The man then reached out another hand to help her regain her footing.

"Quick moves. Thanks." Noel had shaven. The Neanderthal who'd arrived at her door looked more like a model today. He'd traded the denim jacket for a fishermen's sweater over a flannel shirt.

"Are you okay? Did you twist your ankle?"

"I'm fine. Just klutzy." She could feel the heat in her cheeks. She must be fire engine red by now.

"Well, I'm glad you're okay. Can I carry these for you?"

"Sure. They're going right over there to the baked goods booth." She pointed toward it.

As she followed him over there, she couldn't help noticing his muscular physique. He turned around and faced her after putting down the trays. He smiled, and she noticed he had a dimple on one side. Why hadn't she noticed that he was handsome before? Probably because he was so irritating. Today he was acting like a gentleman, so she'd treat him like one. "Thanks for the help. And for keeping me from falling on my face."

"Right place and right time, I guess."

"Yes, well, thanks again."

"Do you have to work all day and night at this thing, or do you get time off?"

"I'll be working the baked sale booth from

noon until five, but then I'll be free."

"Do you want to hang out later? Take some time to enjoy the festivities?"

She hesitated, then shrugged. "Sure, I guess."

"An enthusiastic yes if I ever heard one. I'll meet you back here at five." Great. She wouldn't even have time to freshen up.

With the constant flurry of activity, the time passed quickly. Before she knew it, she was down to five minutes. She removed her apron and smoothed down her sweater. Then she wiped icing off her knee-high leather boots before grabbing a tiny mirror from her purse. She tried to finger comb her hair and put on a coat of lip gloss.

"You don't need that stuff."

"What stuff?"

"Lipstick. Makeup."

"I didn't realize you were standing there. It's just gloss, I don't wear any other makeup."

"Well, you don't need that either."

"Says you."

"You ready?"

"As I'll ever be." No, she wasn't ready. She'd never be ready to spend time with this man. Why was she doing this? She should fake a headache and go home. No. He lived next door. He'd likely insist on driving her.

He took her by the elbow to guide her gently in the direction he wanted to go, and then he released her. Strange that it should feel like a loss. The first place he wanted to stop was the petting zoo. He even bought some carrots, so she could feed the goats and sheep. Then it was on to the 4-H exhibits. The man was an animal lover. That definitely earned him points in her book. If only she was ready for a relationship. She wasn't.

At the cotton candy booth, they ran into Clive. "Clive. This is my tenant, Noel."

"Nice to meet you." He turned to Holly, and she saw the laughter in his eyes. "I'm glad to see you out enjoying yourself, sweetie."

"I'm surprised to see you unchained from your desk this early in the evening."

"Fall festival only happens once a year, and I must have a caramel apple from Candy."

"Have fun but behave yourself."

He leaned in and kissed Holly on the cheek. "Not going to happen, sweetie. I'll see you later."

They watched as Clive sauntered away in search of his prey. "He seems awfully familiar."

"We've been friends since kindergarten. Elementary school sweethearts."

Noel laughed. "That explains it."

Hours flew by as they wandered from booth to booth, and she introduced him to old friends. It was surprising to her how many people knew his name and had his read his books. He seemed too young to have made a name for himself. "How old are you, anyway?"

"I'm thirty. Where did that come from?"

"I don't know. I guess I was thinking about how many people said they knew your novels, so I wondered how long you'd been writing."

"I could pretend I don't know how old you are, but I'm sure you saw me talking to Norma

Jean earlier and you know that I now know the ages and status of every single woman in this town and the neighboring towns for twenty miles in every direction."

"I'll bet you do." She chuckled. "So, a younger man. I'm not sure about being on a date with a younger man."

"Is this a date?" He looked into her eyes as if searching for an answer.

"Not really. Just two acquaintances hanging out."

"I'd like to change that. How about a real date? Say tomorrow night?"

"I don't know. I'm not sure I'm ready for that."

"Sure, you are. I'll pick you up at seven. Let me walk you to your car. It's only nine o'clock, but this place is quickly becoming a ghost-town."

"I should stay and clean up."

"Nah." He looked over at the baked sale booth. "Looks like they've got it under control. You've been here all day. Take a break."

She wanted to argue, but then again, she didn't. She needed to rest her feet. It had been a long day in her new boots. He opened her car door for her and waited for her to get safely inside. She started the engine and watched as he walked over to his Mercedes. Why was a man driving what looked like a brand-new Mercedes staying at her little place on Lake Bethel?

He pulled on a sweater over his t-shirt. Casual seemed the way to go. Why was he even doing this? This stay was about writing, not dating. His editor would have his head if he knew. Well, he could call this a research date. He'd decided to use many of Holly's personality traits for his heroine. There was a soft side to this woman. She wanted him to believe she was hard as steel, and she was, but she was more than that. It was time to get to know her other side.

When he arrived at her door, she opened it before he knocked.

"I'm not doing this," she said.

"Sure, you are."

"No, I'm not."

"Why not? I don't bite."

"I'm not ready to date."

"Then we won't call it a date. Just two ac-quaintances hanging out, same as last night," he said.

"I'm not ready."

"You look ready to me." He looked her up and down. Wow, she did look amazing, espe-cially for someone who wasn't trying."

"Come in and sit down. I'll get ready, but this isn't a good idea."

"I'm sure we've both done things we thought were bad ideas that worked out okay."

"I don't know about that."

She left the room and he thought over what he'd said to her. This was a date and he'd make sure she knew it by the end of the night. He'd need to ease her into the idea. Holly came back into the room with her hair braided and lip gloss on. She didn't need the makeup, but the braid was a cute look. He had an urge to scoop her up in his arms and carry her back to his place, but he knew she wouldn't go for that plan. This was a wedding night kind of girl. Where had that thought come from?

He reached for her hands and took them into his larger ones. "I'm not going to bite. I promise. We'll have a nice time and I'll bring you home in one piece."

"I know. It's not my physical safety I'm worried about. I haven't been out with a man since my husband died. I don't want to dishonor his memory."

"How is it dishonoring? Never mind. Don't answer that. Let's take this one step at a time. We're two friends grabbing a bite to eat. He'd be okay with that, I think, right?"

"Yes. I'm sure he would."

"Then, let's go."

They settled into the car, and he pulled out of the driveway. He had Sirius on and set to Southern gospel. She was clearly enjoying it, since she reached over and turned the volume up. Forty-five minutes later he pulled into the parking lot of the Bloomsburg restaurant. It came highly recommended. It was the first place he'd seen with tablecloths and linen napkins since he'd arrived in the area. The host sat them. After they made small talk over appetizers, Holly appeared more relaxed.

He was surprised when she asked a question that was sure to start a deeper conversation. "What made you decide to start writing?"

"I'm not sure if it was a conscious decision. One night I sat down at my laptop and words just started flowing. The next thing I knew, I'd written fifteen thousand words."

"That's incredible."

"It hasn't happened since. I struggle to get a thousand words written in a sitting."

"Do you enjoy it?"

"Sometimes. Oftentimes, I don't. Yet, I have a need in my soul to craft stories, so I write."

"That's interesting."

"So, why did you decide on baking?"

"It wasn't always baking. I went to school and got my MBA."

"Wow. Impressive. But why not move to the city and work for a big corporation? Why baking?"

"Kevin and I got married after graduation. We decided we wanted children. So, I was going to wait to start my career until they were old enough to go to school. We tried to conceive for a year before he was killed. After that, I realized that life is short and working for a faceless corporation would never fulfill me."

"How was he killed, if you don't mind me asking?"

"Authorities aren't sure. He may have swerved to avoid an animal. He may have fallen asleep at the wheel. Either way, he went over the ravine. Medical examiner said he was killed instantly."

"I'm sorry."

"It was a long time ago."

"It's obvious the pain is fresh."

"I haven't been able to move on. I'm stuck in a holding pattern. It's like I'm waiting for him to come home to start my life." Holly placed her hands over her face. "I can't believe I told you all of that. I'm sorry. I didn't mean to dump that on you."

He reached out and pulled her hands from her face and held them. "No. I'm glad you told me. If we're going to be friends, we need to be real with each other, right?"

"I guess." There was the ghost of a smile on her face. He was determined to make her smile brighter before the date ended.

When the waitress cleared away their dinner plates, Noel ordered dessert and insisted that Holly do the same. He wanted more time with her and was afraid she wouldn't agree to continue the date once they left the restaurant.

Holly devoured the last bite of her dessert. It was a masterpiece. Everything was chocolate, the mousse, ganache, cake, and shavings. "I'm happy you talked me into this. That was delicious."

"Glad you enjoyed it."

He paid the check and helped her put her coat on. Noel was a gentleman. It was a surprise. She'd expected him to act like a Neanderthal. The restaurant choice had been her first surprise, but his compassion was the real shocker. The image she'd created of him didn't include kindness. He was destroying her perceptions one by one. He guided her by the elbow as they walked to the car. He opened the car door for her again. Nobody else had ever done that for her. Of course, she'd never dated. Her only love was Kevin and they'd been together forever.

Noel didn't start the car right away, he turned toward her. "This was nice."

"It was. Thank you."

"I'm supposed to be concentrating on writing, but I've got you stuck in my head all the time."

"No, you don't. Stop lying."

"You, Miss Holly, are a distraction."

"That's your own fault. I'm not pursuing you."

"True. Feel free to change that anytime."

An awkward giggle escaped. What was she doing here? She had a wonderful time, but this was crazy. A man was the last thing she needed in her life. Especially one who would leave soon after Christmas. All she was to him was a way to pass time when he wasn't writing.

"Have I told you that you made it into my book? Not you exactly, but some of your traits."

"You put me in your book without my permission?"

"No. I adapted some of your traits to fit my character."

"Take me home."

"Don't be silly. This isn't a big deal. I thought you would enjoy being immortalized in a character."

"Take me home."

"Are you seriously angry that I used your feisty personality for my character?"

"I'm beyond angry."

"More of that feistiness. I'm not sure I understand what you're upset about."

"And that right there is your biggest problem.

Was all this attention for research purposes? Did you plan to put my grief in there too?"

"No. Of course not. I wouldn't do that. I know how intensely personal that conversation was. I would never use it."

"But I am research."

"I didn't say that."

"I repeat for the third time. Take me home."

She sat staring out the window kicking herself. Why was she being so nasty? She reached for the volume control to turn down the radio so she could apologize, but it was then she saw a phone number scribbled in pink sitting in his console. In plain view. Candy. He wasn't serious after all. Candy could have him. She turned back to the window and resumed her pouting. The forty-five-minute drive dragged on for what seemed like hours.

She didn't wait for him to come around the car. She jumped out and slammed the door. Her house was unlocked, as always, but when she got inside, she bolted the lock behind her before sliding down to the floor and pulling her knees to her chest. There she sat sobbing until she had no tears left. She didn't know what bothered her more, that he used her in his book or that he might be seeing Candy. She didn't own him. They were petty things, but they triggered a torrent of emotion. If only she could figure out why he affected her so strongly.

Holly saw Norma Jean coming and cringed inwardly. There was no way to avoid her now that eye contact was made.

"I'm so glad I caught you before you could sneak out."

"What's up?" Holly asked.

"We need your help for the Christmas pageant. You did so much for the fall festival, and I knew you would want to work on the pageant too."

"I don't know. I'm crazy busy with baking for the holidays. I don't see how I could find time for both. Maybe next year, if I can afford an assistant by then."

"Oh, you're not getting out of it that easy. I talked to Kaitlin, and she said she'd be happy to help you bake your little cupcakes, so that you can make yourself available for the pageant."

"Kaitlin? You think she can do my job? She's sixteen."

"No, silly. I don't mean that she can do your job. I mean she can help you. Be an assistant for a few weeks, so you can be on the pageant committee."

"I guess I'll do it. I shouldn't be agreeing to this with all the orders I have piling up."

"You won't regret it. This is for the Lord. One never regrets things they do for the Lord."

The sentiment might be true, but it was pure manipulation. Why did they rope her into everything? Maybe she should move somewhere where nobody knew her and start over. Dream on. This was home. Her parents' home. Was it really her home?

"When does the committee meet?"

"We start right away. We're running out of time. Tomorrow. First thing."

"I can't do anything first thing. I'm baking for deliveries."

"What time is your last delivery?"

"Nine o'clock."

"Then come by right after. We're starting at nine, so you won't be too late."

"Fine. See you then."

"Wonderful, wonderful, wonderful. I'm so excited you agreed to help. I cannot wait to get started." Norma Jean wrapped her in a hug and practically skipped off. How could a woman that age have so much energy?

Holly watched her from the back of the church as she hunted for her next victim. When she saw her corner Noel by the restrooms, she chuckled. There was no way he'd agree to help out. The man only thought of himself.

She made her way to the exit, shook hands with Pastor Chris and his wife, Casey, and headed out to her car.

Once again, she'd agreed to put her life on hold to appease others. She couldn't wait to hear about how Noel reacted to Norma Jean's requests. He probably handled it the way she should've by saying "no." It was so difficult for her to utter that word when people dumped on her. Now she would be overwhelmed again, unless she gave less than her best effort, but she wasn't a slacker, so that was unlikely.

The holiday party rush would start in a week, and she had some massive orders to fulfill. One order was for the power plant's Christmas party in Berwick. She'd told them she didn't deliver that far, but when they told her how many they needed, she made an exception. Was it a mistake? Could she finish the order?

Noel was running out of time to get this book written. He'd spent too much time over the past few weeks thinking about how bad he'd screwed things up with Holly. He paced back and forth. Why was that woman so infuriating? If she wasn't right next door, maybe the words would flow. He should find a new location to write. His editor wouldn't go for that idea.

Clenching his fists at his sides, he stared out the window toward her house. She was probably asleep. He needed to get her out of his head.

He needed to find a way to dispose of the body, something clever, but not undetectable. He sat back down and picked up his laptop. Septic tank wasn't the solution, the chemicals would dissolve it too much and there would be no smell in a concrete tank with a concrete lid. The body might never be discovered there, and the villain had to get caught. But not too quickly. The hero needed time for personal growth on her journey to catching the bad guy. The answer was probably right in front of him. He searched the computer for hours and came up empty. There were lists filled with brilliant ideas, but none of them felt right for this story. Brainstorming wasn't working either. He'd heard of writer's block but had never experienced it. Thought it was a myth. Maybe this was it. Not knowing the next scene. Was it writer's block or a tiny brunette with an attitude problem? Either way, he was stuck. Skipping around the story wasn't his style, so he needed to figure this out.

He grabbed his jacket and headed for the door.

A brisk walk might help. An hour later, he had circled the lake. It was a nice long walk on a crisp night. The same kind of night he was writing about. The full moon cast an eerie glow in the fog coming off the lake. It was too late in the year to be the hunter's moon in real life, but he could have his book take place in October, so that he could include it. All the better for his story. His villain was hunting women in law enforcement. To have that happen the night of the hunter's moon would be poetic.

As he approached the door to his rented house, the answer came. A metal can for burning trash. A burn barrel. Perfect. His villain could drag the body to the burn barrel in the dark of night and burn it. Out in the country where nobody would smell the smoke. Would it work? Would there be enough left to test for DNA? Could the villain lift the body, could he carry it all the way to the burn barrel. If it was dark, he would struggle, but if he had the light of that full moon, maybe. He decided to put the theory to the test.

He'd seen a fifty-pound bag of dog food in the pantry. Why it was there, he couldn't say. Holly didn't have a dog. Maybe whoever lived here before she owned it did. Opening the pantry, he turned on the light and looked around. It was right where he'd thought he'd seen it. There was a hole where mice had gotten into it, but it would work. He'd not seen any evidence of mice, so the bag had been there for some time. Nobody would miss it. He could throw it out after his experiment. No woman would be fifty pounds, so he needed to find something else to make his load heavier. He turned on and off lights as he searched the house, finally he gave up on finding one or two things to fit the bill and grabbed a bunch of small, heavy items and loaded them into bags. He had one full bag of canned goods. He pulled up the dining room rug. After he placed all the items in the center and folded up one end to keep things from falling out, he rolled the rug up. Balancing it on his shoulder, he opened the back door. It wouldn't be easy, but it could be done. He carried the rug across the yard to the burn barrel. Yes, this could work. He leaned the rug up against the barrel and sat down on a nearby bench to think through the rest of the scene.

Chapter 3

Holly heard noise in the yard. She glanced at the clock; it was three o'clock in the morning. What was going on out there? She climbed out of bed and went to the window. There was enough light for her to see a man carrying a rug across the yard and setting it down to lean against the burn barrel. Why would someone be in her yard in the middle of the night, carrying a rolled-up rug? Duh. It was so obvious. Noel's shape and build. He was disposing of a body. Her initial perceptions had been right. Why had she doubted herself? How could she have believed he was kind and gentle.

She reached for the cordless phone and dialed 9-1-1. The dispatcher took her information and sent the state police. Not having local police meant if there wasn't a state trooper nearby, it would be a long wait. By then, if it was Noel out there, he would be back inside. It would be difficult to prove it had been him at all. She couldn't just sit inside while he got away with murder. She had to do something.

She made her way to the kitchen and watched out the window. He was sitting on a bench. Why would he be sitting there instead of burning his "trash?" Maybe he was worried about the smell waking her. There were no other homes nearby. If he intended to make her his next victim, he wouldn't want her to know it. A plan began to form. She went into the den and got her granddaddy's shotgun from the gun safe. She'd stashed the shells in a box in the desk. Holly loaded it and hurried to the front door. Quietly, she made her way through the side yard and snuck up behind him. She held the gun to his back. Pressing the butt of it firmly against her right shoulder, finger off to the side of the trigger, so as not to accidentally pull it.

"Don't move or I'll shoot." Her voice shook.

"Holly, what are you doing?"

When she didn't answer, he turned around and grabbed the barrel. Her finger moved to the trigger. The gun went off, missing him, and the force knocked her backward. She felt a twinge in her shoulder. Ignoring it, she held the gun firm and inspected the huge hole in her burn barrel. He grabbed for the shotgun again.

"Give me that. You're going to kill somebody with that thing!"

She took a step back, still pointing the gun in his direction. "I have to stop you. Hold you until the cops get here."

"What are you talking about? You're crazy."

"I'm the crazy one?" She looked toward the rolled-up rug leaning against the burn barrel.

"Oh. That. I can explain."

"Save it for the cops." She took another step back so he couldn't grab the gun again. She kept it pointed in his direction.

"I'm a writer."

"Not much of an explanation, Noel."

"I'm figuring out a scene. It's dog food and canned goods in the rug. I'm just checking to see if my antagonist would be able to carry the rug by himself with a body rolled up in it. I didn't kill anyone. Can you please put the gun down?"

She circled closer to the rug and lifted the end with the tip of the shotgun. She peered down into the rolled bundle. Huh, he was telling the truth. She lowered the gun.

"The state police are going to have both of our heads when they get here."

"You called the police? Really? I thought we were becoming friends."

"I'm sure you'll understand that I couldn't make nice with a murderer."

"You honestly believed I'd murdered some-one?"

"The evidence was staring me in the face."

"I should've waited until morning and told you what I was doing. But I can't believe you'd think that of me."

"I'll call the cops back, but you know they're

going to come out anyway. They have no choice."

"You should probably put that weapon away before they get here. Don't want them to shoot and ask questions later."

"Do you want to come inside for a cup of coffee while we wait for them?"

"Sure. Unless you want to let me roll you up in the rug and see if my theory works."

The sharp look she gave him left no room for interpretation.

Was she trying to quell her nervous energy? He glanced at the clock as she pulled muffins from the oven. They smelled delicious. It had been nearly an hour and no sign of the state police yet, Holly had assured him that wasn't all that unusual in these parts. As the thought went through his head, he heard a car pull into the drive.

Holly pointed her index finger at him. "Wait here."

He laughed but did as he was told. It took a few minutes for them to join him in the kitchen.

One of the officers turned a chair around straddling it. "A writer, huh?"

"Yep."

"Have I read any of your books?"

"I don't know. Have you?"

"You'd have to tell me who you are for me to know."

"Oh, sorry. I thought Holly had already filled you in on who I was. Noel Ryan."

"I haven't read your books, but my wife has. Stella loves mysteries and suspense."

Noel gave a little smile. "I could give her some autographed copies if you think she'd like them."

"Definitely, but on a social occasion. I don't want it to look like I'm accepting a bribe." He laughed. "This is my partner, Teri." He tapped the tall woman on the shoulder.

She pointed back at her partner. "And he's Jason."

"I didn't already say that?" Jason frowned.

"No. You didn't," Teri said.

Holly poured coffee and put out muffins. Noel watched her intently. She kept rubbing her shoulder. Served her right for almost shooting him. How could she remain so calm? Then it dawned on him that state police were sitting across the table from him. Two of them.

"I was wondering. Since you're out here anyway, can I pick your brain about this book I'm writing? I'll make sure to mention you in my acknowledgments."

"My wife would get a kick out of that. Her mother was a writer. Children's books."

"Cool."

Noel hammered them with questions for about forty-five minutes when they got another call and had to leave.

"You sure you didn't set this up, so you'd have time to interrogate the police?" Holly cleared the table.

"No, but I won't complain that it worked out that way."

"Well, you're welcome to stay as long as you'd like, but I have to get to baking. I have quite a few orders to get out by nine o'clock."

"You start baking this early?" He stood.

"I have to if I'm going to deliver orders fresh every morning."

"Wow. Do you need some help?"

"No. I have a system."

"Okay. I heard 'stay out of my way,' so I'll go home. We can talk more later." He walked up behind her and gently turned her to face him.

"I don't think there's anything more we need to talk about. If you want to talk about the whole big misunderstanding thing, I get it."

"You nearly shot me. You owe me a conversation."

"You woke me up in the middle of the night and I owe you?"

She bit her bottom lip. *Was she nervous? Anxious? Angry?*

He couldn't wrench his gaze away from her lips. "You're cute when you're cross." He leaned in close and slowly kissed her lips. Moving a stray hair behind her ear, he gazed down at her for a long moment before walking out her back door. He hadn't expected kissing her to affect him so strongly.

Holly stared out the window watching as Noel made his way across the yard. The man was infuriating. What was his problem? First, he wakes her up in the middle of the night. Then he grabs at her shotgun. She gets stuck with him while they wait for the police to show. Then he decides to make nice with the cops and talk shop. As if that wasn't enough, he dared take the liberty to kiss her goodbye? Why hadn't she stopped him?

When he got to his door, he looked back at her and winked. The man was unbalanced. She'd made it clear that she wasn't going to get involved. He needed to take a hint. Holly started dumping ingredients into her KitchenAid mixer. If these cupcakes were going to cool enough to ice before delivery, she had to get them in pronto. Then she remembered the pageant meeting. It was going to be a long day.

Two hours later, she was loading cupcakes into her van and headed out for morning deliveries. It would be exhausting dealing with Norma Jean after getting so little sleep. At least she wouldn't have to deal with Noel anymore today.

Deliveries went smoothly, and she hurried to make it to the planning meeting. She'd have to speak up and let them know she didn't have much time to devote to this pageant thing. She'd made an extra batch of cupcakes to bring to the meeting. People expected baked goods whenever they saw her. She didn't like to disappoint them.

Pastor Chris opened the door as she walked up. He must've been watching her through the front windows.

"Holly's here." The pastor scratched his head.

Fred joined them near the door. "But still no Norma Jean. Have you seen her, Holly?" Fred's brow furrowed.

"I haven't. She'd never be late for her own meeting. Did anyone call her?"

"Several times." Fred took his keys out of his pocket. "I'm going to drive over to check on her."

"Do you want me to come with you?" Holly asked.

"No. She'd want you to stay here and get started." He gave her a strained smile before shuffling out the door.

Pastor Chris led the way to the Sunday School room where several people were chatting and pulling costumes out of boxes.

Noel was sitting at a child-sized table with papers in front of him. Norma Jean must've been more persuasive than Holly had thought possible.

"Long time no see, stranger." Noel grinned.

"Good morning. What are you working on?"

"A script I wrote for the pageant at Norma Jean's urging. I've been marking it up with suggestions from the rest of the crew."

"Oh. They've always used the same script.

Doesn't it come right from the Bible?"

"Yes and no. Reading the old script, I can see they've taken liberties with the biblical version, as most churches do, but this one is different. I start it off with two children. One tries to explain the gospel message to the other, but the second child gets tripped up on the God-manifest-in-the-flesh thing, so he gets some of the kids from his Sunday School class to act out the passages, so he can get a better understanding."

"That is different. May I read it?"

"Sure." He handed her the script.

She took it to the secretary's office to read. Absolute silence was necessary for her concentration. She'd expected the script to read like it had been written in a hurry. Something to get Norma Jean off his back, but it was good. Thoughtful. Insightful. Something only someone familiar with God's word could've written. Why hadn't she known that about him? What else didn't she know? It had been her decision not to get to know him better. Why should she care anyway? Maybe Norma Jean had arrived, and she could find out where she fit in on this project.

Her steps echoed in the hall as she walked back to the Sunday School room. When she stepped into the room, the gloomy atmosphere struck her.

"What's the matter?"

"Fred drove over to check on Norma Jean. She was unconscious and lying on the floor. The ambulance will take her to Danville. It's a little farther than Bloomsburg and Wilkes-Barre, but they think she'll get better care there," Pastor Chris explained.

"Let's hope so."

"All we can do now is pray."

The words triggered memories. So familiar. She'd heard them repeatedly last year. Her mother had been hospitalized. They all knew she was dying. Doctors tried to keep her alive with feeding tubes, first a J-tube and then with TPN. It hadn't been enough. Her starvation had been going on longer than anyone realized. She'd hidden her struggles behind a brave facade. Nothing was enough to combat the gastroparesis at that late stage. Not even her prayers. She'd prayed fervently. Fell asleep praying. Woke up praying. Now she'd do the same for Norma Jean. Would it be enough this time? Norma Jean was the closest thing she had left to a mother. Sure, she was a little wacky and drove her batty, but she had a pure heart.

"Why don't you let me help you sit down?" Noel reached for her arm.

She pulled away from him. "Why don't you leave me alone?"

"Hey, no need to be testy. I'm on your side. I can drive you to the hospital. I don't think you should be driving yet."

"I can drive. I'm fine."

"Holly, Let Noel drive you. He's absolutely correct. You shouldn't be driving."

She wanted to bite back a nasty retort at Pastor Chris, but she kept her mouth shut. Sending up a prayer for a quiet spirit.

Pastor Chris continued. "I would take you, but I have to stay here. I have counseling appointments I don't have time to cancel. I'll be there in about two hours."

As much as she wanted to argue, she knew there was no point. They'd win in the end. Besides, they were right. She shouldn't be driving. Her whole body shook. Was it anger? Fear? She wasn't sure.

Noel stared straight ahead as he drove toward Danville. He didn't try to make conversation at first. Holly was clearly distraught, so now was not the time to interrupt her thoughts. After about twenty minutes, she finally spoke.

"Do you think she'll be all right?"

"I wish I had an answer for you."

"I wish they had taken her to Bloomsburg."

"Why is that? I thought the one in Danville was the best hospital in the area?"

"It is."

"Then why wouldn't you want her to go there?"

"It's where I watched my mother die."

"I'm sorry. How long ago did she pass?"

"Last year. December 10th."

"Wow. Poor timing."

"Yes. It is. I had planned on spending the day at home, but then Norma Jean had insisted I do this pageant thing. I'm sure it was on purpose. To get me out of my own head."

"I'm sure she hadn't planned on this."

"No. Of course not. It's all so surreal."

He reached out and took her hand. She didn't fight him. He wanted to tell her everything would be fine but resisted the urge. She must've heard those words many times before her mother passed. People always told the nice lie. Maybe it was better not to say anything. Just to be there.

Silence filled the car again. When they pulled into the parking lot, he turned toward her.

"You ready to go in?"

"'God doesn't give us more than we can handle.' Those words have haunted me for a year."

"People mean well when they say them."

"I know they do, but it's not helpful."

"No. It's not. I've heard those words my-self." He brushed the hair out of her face and kissed her forehead.

After letting himself out, he walked around the car and opened her door. They walked silently to the doors of the hospital. The EMTs would've taken Norma Jean in at emergency. Would she still be there? Checking with nurses confirmed she was in emergency, but they couldn't let them back yet. Family only. They expected to be moving her to intensive care shortly. What did that even mean? Shortly.

Noel watched Holly glance around the room looking for a seat among the myriad group of sick and injured people. "We could take a walk outside while we wait. Then we wouldn't need to find chairs," he suggested.

"Good plan. I hate hospitals."

They walked down the path toward the chil-dren's hospital building. When they neared the end, they saw Fred. He was stubbing out his cigarette and putting it in his pocket. "Hi Fred. It's a non-smoking campus."

"Yes, I know, but I had to have a smoke and didn't want to leave her long enough to go off-campus for one."

"Understandable. Did they let you back there?" Holly asked.

"They did. I have medical power of attorney for her. I guess they figured I was close enough to family." Fred said.

"They said she wasn't awake."

"She's not. Keep praying."

"We will. We're going to take a short walk. Would you ring my cell when they move her to intensive care? Or if she wakes up?" Holly asked.

"Sure."

Fred leaned down and gave Holly an awkward hug. Then he shook Noel's hand.

"Fred must be close to Norma Jean, huh?" Noel asked.

"I think he's her boyfriend. It's hard to tell. They're together most of the time. He lets her boss him around. They're total opposites. He's reticent and Norma Jean is, well, Norma Jean."

It was another hour before they got the call. Noel could only hear Holly's side of the conversation. It sounded like Norma Jean was being moved.

"What's going on?"

"Fred told me they're moving her to intensive care. He said the doctor was going to meet him in the waiting room. He wants me to join him."

"Okay. Let's head in."

"You don't have to stay, you know. Fred can take me home when it's time. Or Pastor Chris when he gets here."

"I'm not going to abandon you here." He thought she looked relieved, which surprised him. Hadn't she been trying to get rid of him since he showed up to rent her house?

"I'm Dr. Mallick." He shook hands with each

of them in turn.

"Mrs. Paulson hit her head. Probably a fall. When she arrived, she was unconscious. She has not regained consciousness. We won't know the extent of the damage the fall caused until she comes out of her coma."

Holly watched the doctor intently. "She's in a coma?"

"Yes. It can happen when someone loses consciousness and isn't treated immediately. I have to tell you; my immediate concern is her heart. A mild heart attack probably led to the fall. The EKG showed heart muscle damage."

"What are you doing for her?" Holly asked.

"We injected a clot dissolving agent. But for now, we're just making her comfortable. She may need angioplasty or a bypass, but I'll leave it to the surgeon to talk to you about that. We'll call him when and if Mrs. Paulson comes out of the coma."

"If? You don't know if she'll wake up?" Fred asked.

"Unfortunately, we never know. Some people come out of it rather quickly. Others never come out. You may go in and see her now, but I would ask that you go in one at a time and that only one of you remain with her."

"Okay, thank you doctor," Holly said. "Fred, why don't you go in first. Noel and I will wait here."

"Thanks, Holly. I'll be back shortly."

Holly turned to Noel. "Thanks for staying."

"Of course. How are you holding up?"

"I'm okay. The shock was too much on the ride over, but I'm okay now. Maybe she'll be all right."

"I hope so. She's a spunky lady. I like her."

"Yes, she is. I had this terrible thought this morning. I dreaded seeing her. She keeps roping me into things I don't want to do and don't have time to do right. I was annoyed with her."

"Your negative thoughts did not cause this."

"I know that, but I feel guilty nonetheless."

"Pray about it. Then you really need to let it go. Otherwise, it will eat you alive."

"I've been meaning to ask you about something. I read your script for the play. I didn't know you were religious."

"I'm not religious. I do have a strong faith in Jesus. I'm born again and bought by His blood."

"I know you go to church, but I didn't think you were saved. You barely ever talk about God."

"Sure, I do. All the time. It seems you and I haven't spent enough time together if you don't know that."

"Maybe. I don't know."

"I haven't heard you talk much about God either."

"I've been fighting my own spiritual battles lately, so that isn't much of a surprise. I'm not over Him taking my mother. I miss her." She had a catch in her voice.

Noel pulled her close and she let the tears flow. It was at that moment Pastor Chris walked into the room. Holly sprung away from Noel.

"How's she doing?" Pastor Chris asked.

Holly replied, "It didn't sound all that promising. She fell, hit her head, and the result is a coma. They think a problem with her heart caused her fall." The words came out sounding clinical. Matter of fact.

Pastor Chris sat beside them and remained silent. She assumed he was praying.

After several minutes, Fred came back in the room. It was her turn to see Norma Jean.

When she got to the room. Holly stood there a long moment. The elderly woman looked frail. She edged around the bed and took Norma Jean's small hand in her own. It was cold. She tried to warm it in her own hands. Then she pulled the blankets up higher. "You better wake up. I'm not ready to lose you too. Please wake up." She perched on the edge of the chair by the bed, staring at her friend. Hoping for some sign of life.

Chapter 4

The waitress came by and filled their cups again. The diner was comfortable. Familiar. They'd stopped on their way back from the hospital. Holly knew she wouldn't eat if she went home, so she'd agreed when Noel had suggested stopping for food. She'd picked at her French toast and nibbled on her bacon, but at least she'd eaten something.

"They're going to throw us out if we don't leave soon," she said.

"The place is nearly empty. I don't think they're worried about us taking up a table. I'll leave her a good tip."

"I'm not ready to go home either."

He smiled tenderly.

Just then her cell rang, and she answered it. "Hello." Holly said.

"Fred? Is that you? You're breaking up." She listened for a few minutes trying to understand him.

Holly set the phone down.

"Bad connection, but I think Norma Jean woke up."

"Well then, I guess you don't have to go home after all. Let's head back to the hospital."

"Are you sure you don't mind?"

"I don't mind at all."

"It'll just be for a few minutes, so I can see for myself that she's awake."

"There is no need to hurry."

Twenty minutes later they strode through the doors of the hospital entrance again.

When they arrived at intensive care, Noel stayed in the waiting area while Holly went in to see Norma Jean. Holly tried to conceal her slight limp until she was sure Noel couldn't see her. She had a tricky hip. It was acting up from too much walking, but she didn't need Noel fussing over her.

She approached the bed slowly. Norma Jean's eyes were closed. Fred sat beside her holding her hand.

"Hi, Fred. Is she asleep?" she whispered.

"Yes, but this time it's just sleep."

Norma Jean's eyes fluttered open. "Holly?"

"Yes, it's me."

"Good. Now go home." It was a relief to hear her voice.

"I'm not leaving you. Not yet anyway."

"Then make him leave."

"I don't think that's going to happen."

Her eyes shut. She was asleep again.

There was only one chair, so Fred rose to let her have it.

"You don't need to get up."

"It's fine. She's sleeping, and I wouldn't mind stretching my legs. I'll be back before long."

She'd heard him speak more words today than in all the years she'd known him. Must be hard to communicate in grunts when dealing with calamities like this.

Time seemed to stand still as she sat next to that hospital bed. She spent the time talking to God. It had been a while. Words didn't come easily, but she poured out her heart.

"I'm sorry, I didn't mean to interrupt." Fred leaned against the door frame.

Holly looked up. "It's okay, Fred. I was praying."

"I've been doing quite a bit of that myself. I don't want to interrupt."

"No, it's okay. I left Noel out there, so I should probably get back to him. I'll come back tomorrow." She stood.

Fred walked over and gave her an awkward hug. "Okay, see you then."

"Make sure to get some sleep, okay?"

"Sure. The nurses will bring me a cot."

"You should go home, but I won't argue the point."

"I appreciate that. Maybe I'll go home for a few hours when you come back tomorrow."

"Sounds like a plan."

The drive home was a quiet one. It was an exhausting day for them both. Tomorrow would be similar for Holly. Noel wished he could do more to help. He longed to take away her pain.

He drove into the quaint lakeside community and marveled at how empty it felt. Not a soul on the streets. He'd noticed that things shut down early, but it was almost eerie. He drove around the lake and pulled into the shared driveway. It was odd that houses with so much acreage would be right on top of each other. He'd never asked her how she came to own both.

Noel turned in his seat to face Holly. "Hey, mind if I ask you something?"

"Not at all. Shoot."

"How did you wind up owning the house next to yours?"

"My mother died and left it to me." She looked down at her folded hands.

"You lived next door to your mother?" It came out sounding more astonished than he'd intended.

"My husband and I had our house built. We built here, so we could be near my parents. We thought they'd be able to help with the children, when we had them. I never thought I'd end up losing them so soon." She looked up at Noel with moisture in her eyes.

"I know about your mother's death, but what happened to your father?"

"Oh, he's not dead. He left. I guess he couldn't handle Mom's illness."

"Wow. That's tough." He stared straight ahead; jaw clenched. "Have you heard from him?"

"Once. He wanted me to have Mom sign the divorce papers."

"Ouch."

"Some people can't handle illness. My dad is one of those people."

"I'm sorry. I shouldn't have pried." He reached for the door handle.

"No. It's fine. Do you want to come in for a cup of coffee?" Her voice sounded hopeful. It was a promising turn of events.

"I'd like that." He got out of the car and opened her door.

They went in the back door. He'd often wondered why she always used the back door. Maybe because the kitchen was her comfort space and she liked walking into it. It was more likely that she didn't want to track dirt into the living room, but he liked the other explanation.

"Would you start a fire while I dig up some grub and make coffee?"

"Sure. Where do I get the wood?"

"There's kindling by the fireplace and just outside that side door on the screen porch is a pile of wood."

He gathered up some logs and began laying the fire. It was roaring by the time Holly came back.

"I brought scones and coffee."

"Sounds heavenly."

They once again fell into a comfortable silence.

The pageant planning committee held an emergency meeting called by Pastor Chris. Noel thought it was a great idea. He'd driven in by himself since Holly was making deliveries. This time they'd pushed the meeting to ten o'clock, so she could be there for the start. Noel had arrived early. He glanced up at the clock. It was two minutes until ten. The committee members were assembled around the conference table, drinking coffee and waiting for Holly.

As if on cue, the front door swung open and Holly breezed in, pumpkin rolls in hand. Was that woman ever without baked goods? She set the tray on the table, reached into her bag and pulled out a knife. He was surprised when she handed it to him. He had no idea how to cut a pumpkin roll. After he sufficiently butchered one of the pumpkin rolls, Pastor Chris took the knife and deftly cut the other. Noel got up and fixed Holly a cup of coffee. Before long, plates were passed around the room, and everyone was enjoying the bounty.

Pastor Chris rose and walked to the black board. He made a list of things that needed to be done, then turned to face the planning committee. "Thanks for coming in. As you know, our Norma Jean will be unable to head up any more planning committees for a while. When she's released, which she is hoping is in time to see the pageant, she will need to rest, so we'll need to pull together to stay on top of her responsibilities. As most of you know, she can be persuasive and talk people into 'volunteering.' She 'volun-told' me to be here today, and it was suggested that I 'tell' Holly to volunteer for the director position."

"Oh no! When will I find the time without running my baking business into the ground?"

"We'll all help with the details. Your job will be to tell us what to do. I promise you we'll do as we're told," Pastor Chris said.

"Yeah, right!"

"No, really. This time we'll try. And if you need help making deliveries, Casey said she'd make deliveries for you until the new year. Will you do this for us?" Pastor Chris asked.

Noel wanted to bail her out. Say he'd do it, but he didn't belong here, it wasn't his town, and it wasn't his place to rescue Holly. It would most likely annoy her rather than be helpful.

"Fine. I'll do it, but I don't want any flak from any of you." Holly glared at them, hands on hips.

There were grins around the table as the tiny brunette made her threats and then started dishing out orders. It seemed they picked the right person after all. She was good at giving direction. Norma Jean would've known that. He was sure that's why she'd suggested Holly in the first place.

Before long, he was at Holly's side while the rest of them bustled around to various locations around the church. One to find costumes, another to find candles, and yet another to pick music. Noel walked up to Holly. "What did you want me to do, boss?"

"Very funny. I want you to stick around for a few minutes in case anyone has script questions. That way they can go directly to you."

"I'm sure you have something I could work on in the meantime."

"Not really." She stared down at her clipboard. "Unless you have musical talent, in which case go find Marissa, she'll get you set up with something to work on."

"I don't know about talent, but I play guitar."

"Good enough. Do you have it with you today?" She looked up at him.

"Nope."

"Do you have it at the house? Can you bring it to the next practice?"

"Sure."

"Perfect. Go work out with Marissa what you'll be playing and then you can get back to your writing for the day, if you want." She looked back down.

"Are you almost done here?"

"Probably. It looks like everyone is clear on their responsibilities."

"I'd offer you a ride home, but I know you have your van. Do you feel like taking a walk around the lake when you get home?"

"It's kind of cold for that, isn't it?" She walked to the blackboard.

"Yes, but it'll be fun."

"Okay. Why not?"

"Great. I'll see you at home." He chuckled to himself. The words made it sound like they lived together.

Holly flew in the door and up the stairs. She was glad that her hip was feeling better, and she could take a walk around the lake with Noel. Why was she going anyway? And why was she changing her clothes for a simple walk? It was just a walk. She didn't need to be cute. Yet, for some reason she wanted to look her best. Finding a peach sweater and stretch jeans that would look good with her high brown boots, she placed everything neatly on her bed and went to fix her hair. She took out the ponytail holder and let her curls bounce freely. Should she clip the front in a barrette? No. It would be fine. When she dressed, she stuck a barrette in the pocket of her jeans, in case the wind blew her hair all over the place. Best to be prepared.

She wasn't surprised to look out her bedroom window and see Noel leaning up against the oak tree waiting for her. She hurried back down and went out to meet him. "Sorry I took so long."

"You didn't take long at all. You're all out of breath."

"I know. I hurried."

"You could've taken all day." He grinned. "I would've waited for you."

"Sure, you would've." The words had a sarcastic lilt to them.

"I would've."

"If you say so."

He held out his gloved hand and she placed hers in it. It surprised her how easily she fell into the habit of allowing such closeness with him. Why was she starting to trust him?

She noticed that he slowed his pace to match hers. A gentleman. Why had she thought he was an ogre?

She reached out a hand and caught a snow-flake. "It's snowing."

"Just a little flurry."

"I hope we get a foot." She stopped walking and glanced up at him.

"Why would you want that?"

"I like to sit inside by the fire and watch it come down."

"Sounds lovely." He started walking again, and she kept pace.

"This town practically shuts down when it snows. It's nice. The neighborhood kids all sled and build snowmen."

"I wonder how you even see the kids outside from your side of the lake. I'm your only neigh-bor."

"I take a quad into town, so I can partake in the fun. Before mom got sick, she would go too. It started when I was young. She would take me to town, so I would have other kids to play with."

"Must be a powerful quad to ride in a foot of snow."

"Oh no. When there was a foot on the ground, we used the snowmobiles."

"Oh. Okay. You two had a plan for everything, huh?"

"Yep."

They slowed their steps when they reached the far side of the lake. Noel stopped and turned to face Holly. Something in the way he gazed into her eyes made her insides tingle. She looked away.

"Do you make snow angels too?"

"I haven't for a long time."

He turned to look out over the frozen lake. The snow was starting to lay on the ground and on the tree branches.

"Do the kids ever ice skate on the lake?"

"Later in the year they do, but it isn't frozen enough yet. If they tried it, it would crack under their weight."

"I figured that. It wasn't frozen yet a few weeks ago."

"Did you grow up near a lake?" She raised a brow.

"No, not really. We'd go to a park called Marsh Creek occasionally. It was about an hour away. A beautiful enormous lake. At least to us kids it seemed large. And there was another park Mom took us to called the Willows. It was named for the willow trees covering the property, but we didn't have a nearby lake. I remember going sledding though. There was a big hill up the street. We had a blast careening down it at top speeds. Although, one year a girl had to be taken to by ambulance when she plowed into a tree at the bottom." He stared out over the frozen lake.

"A friend of mine grew up down that way. She told me they sledded at the high school. Sounds odd to me. I guess when you have hills everywhere, it's hard to picture a place with so few of them."

"Lots of kids sled at the schools down there."

"I attended a junior/senior high. They didn't want the expense of two schools for so few kids. We didn't even have a hill at the school, so sledding would've been a challenge there."

"I never heard of combining junior and senior high. And who still has a junior high, isn't middle school all the rage."

"It's fairly common in these parts. And no middle school."

"You make Lake Bethel sound like another country. You're only three hours from Philadelphia."

"But worlds apart."

"I guess that's true. My childhood home is on the main line. Gladwyne. As close as we were to Philly, our home was on a quiet secluded lot surrounded by trees. It was idyllic. For a suburb, anyway. It wasn't like this." He made a circle with his hands lifted. When he stopped, he met her gaze again.

He took her hand in his and lifted it to his lips, planting a kiss on her leather glove. A giggle escaped.

Noel knocked on the kitchen door but opened it as he did. "Hey. I stopped by to see if I could help with anything." A large dog pounced on him, excited to have a visitor. "When did you get a boxer?"

"Toby's not mine. He's Clive's dog. I'm sitting for him." A pang of jealousy hit him, but he brushed it away. She was dog sitting not sleeping with the guy.

The sight of a young girl with fiery red hair in the kitchen had him lifting an eyebrow in Holly's direction. "I see Toby's not the only new addition."

"Noel, this is Kaitlin. Kaitlin, Noel. Kaitlin is helping me out until New Year's when she must go back to school. She's been going to vo-tech to learn cooking, so she can be a chef. Norma Jean, in her infinite wisdom, thought some experience here might help. I'm glad she suggested it." She turned to face Kaitlin. "The first trick will be learning to tame her curls, so she can keep her hair out of the food." Kaitlin tried to get her hair into a ponytail holder, but the curls sprung out everywhere. Holly giggled. Noel figured she understood the struggle of taming wild curls.

"It's nice to meet you." He held out a hand and Kaitlin shook it with her flour-covered one before going to the sink to wash her hands. Toby bounced over to get attention. He scratched behind the dog's ears.

"What are we baking today?"

"Cupcakes, as usual, but also coffee cake, muffins and cookies. It's a busy day."

"Do you need me to run orders anywhere?"

"No, Casey is coming by to deliver today's orders. Aren't you supposed to be writing a book, mister?"

"Yes, but procrastinating can be more fun."

"I'll bet."

He moved closer to her. "It's especially fun when procrastinating involves an adorable baker."

"Flattery doesn't work on me. Have a seat." She turned to Kaitlin. "We can afford to take a short break."

Kaitlin grabbed the coffee pot. Toby did his best to knock her down running between her legs, but she remained upright.

Holly looked pointedly at Noel. "But after coffee all three of us need to get back to work."

"Yes, Ma'am." He faked a southern drawl.

Holly took a coffee cake from the oven and set it on the table with a knife. He made no move for it remembering the disaster with the pumpkin roll. Kaitlin poured coffee for all three.

"Aren't you a little young for coffee?" he asked.

"No. Dad made me wait until I was fourteen to have it, but I drink it regularly now."

"I don't think my parents let me have coffee at fourteen," he said. "What about you, Holly?"

"I think I did. I can't remember life before coffee."

"What are you writing this week? Any exciting plot twists?" Holly asked.

"You'll have to wait for the book like everyone else."

"Nope. I call foul. You don't get to bring imaginary bodies into my yard for burning and then refuse to fill us in on the storyline."

Kaitlin choked on her coffee. "Wait. What?" she sputtered out when she regained her voice.

"He brought a rolled-up rug into the backyard in the middle of the night because he wanted to see if it was plausible for his character to carry a body that way."

"Wow. You must take that writing stuff seriously?" Kaitlin said.

"I do."

"Does it pay well?" Kaitlin asked.

Noel laughed. "I do all right."

"If the Mercedes in the driveway is any indication, he does fine." Holly said.

"Why stay here then? Why not some big fancy house on a private lake somewhere?" Kaitlin asked.

"First off, I'm not rich. Second, I stayed in Lake Bethel a few times as a child with my grandfather. I wanted to come back."

"And I had the only house for rent on the lake, so you ended up here."

"That's how it went down, yes."

"I've got to get back to these cupcakes. They aren't going to frost themselves. Kaitlin, do you want to learn some tricks for decorating Christmas cupcakes?"

Kaitlin rose from her chair and strode to the counter. It wasn't long before Holly handed off the task to her and walked back over to Noel. "I think you have some writing to do."

"Fine. Fine. I'll go." He stood, stretched and then pulled at her hand to indicate he wanted her to walk him out. Toby followed.

"Can I see you tonight?"

"I don't know. Things are busy and I'm not sure about this." She pointed to him and back at herself. His heart raced when her hand came to rest on his bicep. "Your lease is up soon." The words sounded strained.

He nodded. Holly stood on her tiptoes and kissed him gently. She was moving closer physically while putting up emotional barriers. Was that what she wanted? For his lease to be up? For him to leave. The pain gave him a jolt. He hadn't realized how much it mattered.

Chapter 5

Holly saw Noel walk into rehearsal carrying his guitar. He hadn't asked if she wanted to drive in with him, so she'd driven herself, arriving right on time. She was surprised he was late. It was a first in the brief time she'd known him.

She walked over to him. Her stomach betrayed her with little flips. "Hey, stranger. What's going on?"

"Nothing."

"It's not like you to be late?"

"No, I guess not."

"And you don't want to elaborate?"

"Not really, no." She wondered why he was being so evasive. There was definite tension. She didn't know how to break it.

"Okay, then I guess we should head into the auditorium and get started on rehearsal."

"Why do you refer to it as an auditorium?

Don't most churches call it a sanctuary?" He sounded annoyed. Why would he care what they called their church? It didn't make sense.

"Yes, most do call it a sanctuary, but the Bible says the believer is the sanctuary. Believers make up the church, so this is a building like any other and Pastor Chris is adamant that we shouldn't refer to it as something it isn't."

"I guess that makes sense."

They walked over in silence. She wasn't sure what Noel was upset about, but something was obviously bothering him. Had she done something to offend him? She spent the next hour assisting the children with their lines, talking with Marissa about the music, and supervising the finishing touches on the set. The busyness made it possible for her to push Noel to the back of her mind, even though he was in the same room. She didn't have the time to fret over his moodiness.

When the rehearsal ended, she found him waiting outside for her, so she confronted him. "So, what's with you today?"

"What do you mean?"

"You're different."

"You're imagining things. Do you want to go to the diner and grab a bite?"

"I guess."

"We'll take my car and pick yours up after."

"Okay."

He held the door for her, as usual. She was learning to expect the courtesy.

Whatever was bothering him, he seemed to have put it aside. He was back to his usual charming self. Maybe he was struggling with his writing. She'd heard writers were a moody bunch.

He leaned back in the booth and closed his eyes briefly. "My family is coming in for Christmas."

She grinned. "That's fabulous. Your mom and dad?"

He sat up straight. "All of them. My sister planned it without checking with me first. They know I'm supposed to be writing, but apparently 'I blew off' Christmas last year because I was writing. Sally isn't going to let that happen again."

"How does one 'blow off Christmas'?" She raised an eyebrow.

"I didn't. I went to my parents for Christmas dinner. Sally's crazy. She thinks because I didn't spend the entire week celebrating with them that it wasn't enough."

"A little controlling, huh?"

"That she is."

"Is she the oldest?"

"No, believe it or not she's the youngest. Of nine."

"Wow. Nine?"

"Yep. And they're all coming here. Where am I going to fit ten people?" He sighed.

"Good luck with that."

"I don't believe in luck."

"In that case, I'll be praying for you. There's a bed and breakfast not far from here. Maybe they have room?"

"Booked. I called and asked when Sally told me they were coming."

"Your sisters could stay at my place."

"You'd quickly grow to regret that offer. They'll have to squeeze. We'll have sleeping bags and air beds strewn from one end of the place to the other."

"If you change your mind. Let me know."

"If I change my mind, I'll send them over." He chuckled.

"When do they arrive?"

"Saturday, December 23rd. Then they'll stay for Christmas Eve, Christmas Day and head home the day after."

"I think it's great. It would be amazing to have family who want to spend the holidays with you enough to go to all that trouble."

"I guess." He sighed.

"Do you think we're ready for the pageant?" She picked at her nails.

"We better be. Next Friday will sneak up on us fast."

"I'm sure it will."

"It's a shame my family won't make it here

in time for the pageant." He laughed.

"I'm sure if you'd told them about it, they'd be here."

"They would. That's why I didn't tell them."

"You about ready to get out of here?"

"Not unless I can talk you into shopping with me. I need to pick some things up to make it feel like Christmas or my family will have a fit that the house is undecorated."

"They will, huh?" She tilted her head.

"Absolutely."

"Sure, I'll go with you."

Holly enjoyed the afternoon of shopping with Noel. She'd tossed Christmas decorations that struck her fancy into his cart and when he raised an eyebrow, she'd stick out her bottom lip in a pout and he'd let her get it. Before long they had enough to decorate his place and possibly the rest of the lakeside community. She rested her eyes while he drove them back to the church to get her van. Then she drove them both to a tree farm where they cut down two six-foot-tall trees. She let him lug them to the van.

After setting up the tree, he started pulling decorations out of the bags. He found some candles with holders and tried to set them up on the dining room table.

"No. No. I'll take care of that. You don't know what I'd planned to do with them," Holly said.

"Okay. What should I do?"

"Why don't you put the lights on the tree?"

"We have to let the branches settle overnight." He didn't know if it was true, but his father had always said it.

"Okay. Then maybe you could make cocoa."

He laughed. Obviously, she wanted him out of the way while she decorated. She'd grown up in this house, so she probably had a clear vision of what it should look like. He trudged into the kitchen to make the cocoa. He'd probably mess that up too, but it allowed him a few minutes to escape the intoxicating scent of lilacs that made him want to pull her into his arms. He'd save that for after the decorating.

Wandering into the living room, he set the two cups of cocoa on the coffee table.

"Yum. Whipped cream."

"Do you like it?"

"I do, but I shouldn't have it if I'm going to maintain my girlish figure."

He chuckled. She didn't have to worry about her figure. "You can afford the whipped cream." He lifted his eyes back up to her face.

"Is it starting to look like Christmas in here?" Holly asked.

He inspected the room. "It sure is. Sit with me a minute."

She sat on the other end of the couch. He inched closer to her until their legs were touching. Holly giggled.

"Has anyone ever told you how beautiful you are?" he asked.

"My mother, and my husband."

"Let me add myself to that list. You're absolutely beautiful, Holly Ewing."

"Thank you. You're not so bad yourself. Ruggedly handsome, I'd say."

"Would you?" He felt a vein in his neck pulsing. This woman would be his undoing.

He kissed her. She leaned into the kiss, and he had to force himself to end it. Seeing her with swollen lips and scratched face from his day-old stubble was too much for him. With a deep intake of breath, he stood. He had to get out of the room before they took things beyond where either of them was ready to go. After gathering his wits, he carried what was left of their cocoa back to the kitchen. He thought back to her comments the other day about how little time he had left on his lease. Did she still want him to leave? Was she feeling any of what he was? He ran his fingers through his hair and stared out the kitchen window, praying for answers.

Holly tried to affix the star to the top of the six-foot tree. It wouldn't stay in place, so she tried pushing branches in it to hold it. The ladder teetered. She flailed her arms but couldn't regain her balance. Pain gripped her. It was a familiar pain. Staying put, she wondered how she would get help. A giant ball of fur bounced in. Toby laid down beside her, tongue lapping at her face. How had she forgotten she was dog-sitting Toby? How could she dog sit with a dislocated hip? Clive had already left town for his Christmas cruise. There was no choice. She'd agreed to take care of him. Maybe Kaitlin could help. Speaking of her, if she could get to the telephone, she'd come help. That girl was a God-send. She thanked the Lord that she'd accepted Norma Jean's suggestion to hire her on, despite her initial trepidation.

She pushed herself along the floor toward the telephone. Tears filled her eyes as she felt bone grind against bone. How could she be so careless? When, at last, she made it to the phone, it was not Kaitlin's number that she dialed. It was Noel's. She barely uttered the words "I fell," when she heard him crash out of his house. Moments later he was kneeling at her side. Toby pounced on him, kissing his face.

"You really should lock your doors," he said.

"I live in the country. And, at the moment, I don't need a lecture on door locks. Are you going to help me, or not?" She spoke through gritted teeth.

He reached down to pick her up and she flinched at the movement.

He raised an eyebrow. "I'm going to carry you out to the car. We'll get you to the ER. Okay?"

She nodded. "Thank you for coming."

"No argument. You must be in a lot of pain."

She grimaced.

He settled her into the passenger seat and then he pushed the seat back as far as it would go, so she would have room to adjust. His closeness was electrifying despite the pain. It was too much to take in. She twisted away from him, wrenching her left hip more. A cry of pain escaped, and he leaned over her again to help her. Boy, did that move backfire.

"Is that better?" he asked after helping her to

adjust the back of the seat.

It wasn't, the adjusted seat only made matters worse, so she lied. "It's fine." She winced involuntarily, but then smiled to convince him she was indeed fine.

He looked skeptical, but he walked around the car and got in the driver's side. She closed her eyes and tried to ignore the pain.

She gave him directions to get to the hospital and he sped down Route 487 toward Bloomsburg. In a short thirty minutes, they'd arrived. Fifteen minutes sooner than they would've if she'd been the one driving.

He hurried around the car, opened her door and bent down to pick her up, but she interrupted the action. "If you go inside, they have wheelchairs."

"Okay. I'll get you one." He wasn't gone more than two minutes when he came back with a wheelchair big enough to fit five of her. He'd clearly grabbed the first one and hadn't considered the size. She accepted his help into the monstrous chair. A few minutes later, she was checking in.

The elderly woman working at check-in smiled. "Sorry to see you back, Holly. What'd you do this time?"

"Dislocated my hip."

"Again?"

"It's the first time in months, but this one is bad. I can't put it back in myself. And it's the left instead of the right this time."

"We'll get you in to see the on-call doctor."

"Thanks, Jan."

"Sure, hon. Take a seat in the waiting room. It shouldn't be more than a couple of minutes."

Noel wheeled her into the adjoining room and turned her around, so they could sit together and talk. "Do you do this often, Holly?"

"No. This is the first time the left hip has gone out. I dislocate the right hip sometimes, but not often."

He took in a quick breath. "Okay. Well, hopefully the doctor can fix you right up."

Holly knew they were in for a long night, imaging would be done, doctors would talk about her within her earshot, and eventually, they would help her get the hip back in place before sending her on her way. It was her normal. It had been her mother's normal. She hadn't found a doctor who could tell her why she had these problems. One had suggested hypermobility once.

A nurse came back to take her into triage. Noel stayed with her.

In the wee hours of the morning, she remembered Toby. They didn't let him out before they left, and he'd had a full bowl of food and water. She would be in for a mess when she got home. Cleaning up after Toby would be a challenge. She'd ask Kaitlin and her parents if she could stay at the house for a few days.

Noel knocked once to let Holly know he was there and then sauntered in. He was early, arriving before Kaitlin came to help with the baking. That way he'd have a few minutes to talk to Holly alone.

"Holly?" he called out.

"In here." He followed the sound of her voice to her pantry. She was gathering supplies, but the grimace on her face made it clear that she was in considerable pain.

"May I help you?"

"Yes." She offloaded the armful of supplies into his waiting arms and then reached for more. He took them to the kitchen counter, but hurried back, so she wouldn't try to carry things in herself.

"These canisters are heavy. Did you ever consider keeping them handy on your counters?"

"I have, yes. But I don't want my kitchen to look messy when my neighbor shows up unannounced," she said with a teasing lilt to her voice.

"You ought to be grateful this neighbor stopped by, as it would've taken you quite some time to get all of those supplies together while hobbling along with your cane."

"I don't hobble."

"Oh, yes you do." He grinned. "It's the cutest hobble I've ever seen."

She threw a dish towel at him. "I'm never going to get today's orders done."

"Sure, you are. I'm here to help and Kaitlin will be here in an hour. Is Casey still doing the driving?"

"She is."

"Then it's under control. I was hoping we could talk while we worked. Show me what to do and I'll do it." She gave him measuring cups and bowls and had him measure the flour into each bowl. Meanwhile she worked on adding spices. He didn't know how she kept straight what she was mixing in each bowl.

"So, what do you want to talk about?"

"What the doctor said last night."

"Which thing?" she asked.

"When he did the biopsy. He said you might have some weird genetic thing, it started with an 'e', I think."

"He wrote it down for me, so I could look it up. What about it?"

"Aren't you worried?"

"I haven't processed the idea yet. I give him credit for at least trying to find an answer and suggesting a possibility. Most doctors dismiss my symptoms since they aren't easily connected."

"You understood the word 'incurable', right?"

"I did." She laughed. "I've been dealing with whatever is wrong with me my whole life. There was a time I thought my symptoms were normal, that everyone suffered from chronic pain and dislocations. My mom dealt with the same stuff. Having a name for it won't change much. If anything, it will add legitimacy to my health complaints."

"Okay. I thought you would be more upset, and I wanted to be there for you if you needed me."

"It may hit me later, but for now, I'm fine."

"Yes, you are *fine*, Miss Holly." He stepped around the counter and took the spoon from her hand. He set it on a plate. He gathered her up in his arms and carried her to the living room sofa.

"Why have you absconded with me?"

He ignored the question until he'd set her down on the couch and settled in beside her. The air was electric between them. "Kaitlin will be here soon, and I didn't want her to walk in on a private moment." He whispered.

"What makes you think I want a private moment with you?" Her voice came out huskier than usual.

"This does." His lips grazed hers.

Her arms went around his neck, and she pulled him closer. The kiss deepened.

There was a growl deep in her throat. He didn't want to let go. So, instead, he pulled her to him and held her for a long moment.

When he released her, he reached up and removing her hair band, freed her curls to fall around her face. "You are gorgeous." He leaned down and kissed her again. It was time to back off and give her some space, but he couldn't break the spell.

"You're the attractive one." There was a

crack in her voice. He could see the vulnerability in her eyes. She wasn't pushing him away this time.

As he leaned down to steal another kiss, the door opened.

"Holly?" Kaitlin called.

Toby stared up at them and let out a bark. He could swear the dog felt his pain.

Holly stood by the altar, leaning on her cane, watching the people file into the church, candles in hand. *Joy to the World* was playing over the sound system. The atmosphere seemed charged with Christmas spirit. There was something about this time of year that brought out something special in people. She hurried backstage to make sure the pageant cast was ready. She'd run through lines with the cast earlier. The biggest part was the angel. The little boy with the golden hair had memorized his lines at the first practice. He was prepared and ready to go. So, Holly concentrated on helping the other little ones.

Joseph, Mary, the shepherds, the sheep, and the donkeys. All seemed prepared. They didn't have an infant, so a baby doll was used as a stand-in for baby Jesus.

And, of course, two teen boys would start the pageant. The one would ask the other to explain what Christmas had to do with Jesus and then the Christmas story would play out while the teen explained the true meaning of Christmas. Noel had written a fantastic script. She caught Norma Jean's eye when Fred helped her find a seat near the front. Norma Jean smiled and gave a little wave. It was so good to see her out and about. Holly had butterflies in her stomach. It was time.

She hobbled up to the stage. "Good evening. Welcome to Lake Bethel Bible Church. We have a fun-filled pageant prepared for you. I'll turn it over to Pastor Chris now." Holly went backstage to check that the musicians were ready. They were up next. She wished that she'd been gifted with musical talent, but she hadn't learned to play an instrument and her vocals were mostly off key, so she settled for singing in the car with the windows up.

Holly made it back in time to see Pastor Chris close his Bible after the scripture reading. The music started. The violin was the first to play the strains of *O Little Town of Bethlehem,* then the curtains opened, and the piano joined in, followed by the choir. She felt as if her heart would explode. The love of Christ was palpable. Sometimes she wished Christmas lasted all year long. Her mom had felt the same way. The thought brought a tear to her eye, but she wouldn't let the pain of her loss ruin this special day. She tucked away the thought for later and focused on the music.

When the music ended the teen boys came up from the front row and sat down on the edge of the stage. It almost seemed unrehearsed, natural.

She sat in a folding chair and let herself get lost in the story. Well, until the angel came out on stage and froze. He couldn't speak. Stage fright? Before she knew what was happening, Noel stepped in. He took a microphone from the piano and spoke the angel's lines into it. There was a round of laughter from the congregation as they realized what was happening, but the show went on without any further complications.

Near the end of the service, she got choked up at the sight of Noel sitting beside the teen boys, playing his guitar as the three of them sang *The First Noel.* Her heart swelled. It was then she realized with dismay that she only had a few more days. He was leaving. He didn't know how she felt about him. Did he feel the same? Would he rush home and never look back? What if he didn't have feelings for her? Maybe she'd been nothing more than a distraction? Something to do while away from home. So much for the warm feelings of Christmas.

A rush of heat rose to her face when she realized the song was over and she was supposed to be on stage. She trudged up the steps. When she finally got the microphone, she straightened her shoulders and held her head high. She might be mortified, but she didn't have to look like it.

"Thank you for joining us for our annual pageant. I'd like to thank Noel Ryan for writing the script and praise God for giving us the most important parts. Everyone laughed. We hope you've been blessed by our young people and the message they shared tonight. Please join us in making a circle around the perimeter of the room. We will light our candles as we sing *Silent Night*. Please dim the lights, deacons."

The lights were dimmed, and the violin started playing. Noel stood beside her and put his arm around her shoulders. The faint masculine scent of his cologne tickled her nose. He gazed down at her, and they made eye contact. She felt like the only woman in the room. Pastor Chris lit the first candle and from there he lit Noel's. Slowly little lights filled the room until there was a warm glow. It was beautiful sight. Holly was ready for Christmas. She wanted this Christmas to last forever.

Chapter 6

Noel heard the SUV pull up and went out to greet his family. They were all there, except for his older brother, Nathan, and his wife, Jenna, who would be driving down from upstate New York. "I can't believe you're all here. I still don't know where you're going to sleep."

"We brought sleeping bags." Samantha chimed in. He gave hugs all around and showed them into his temporary home.

The men carried in the bags while the women congregated around the kitchen table.

Noel's father slapped him on the back. "Son, you couldn't have picked a better place to spend Christmas."

His mother joined in. "This place is beautiful. Pine and spruce covered with snow. It's idyllic."

"Yes, it is. Isn't it?" He'd been spending most of his time concentrating on the view next door, not the one outside.

Sally said, "This place looks amazing. Looks like a woman decorated it."

"She did. My landlady, Holly."

"Really, did that service come with the rent?"

"No. She helped me out as a friend."

"Some friend," Sally said.

They admired Holly's decorating skills for a few minutes before settling into the living room. Sally and Stephanie sat on the floor by the fireplace. The rest of them crowded onto the sparse furnishings.

"Are you going to start a fire, Noel?" Stephanie asked.

"Sure. If you want me to."

"I do," Sally chimed in.

He knelt and got the fire started. When he rose to his feet, he stood over his mother. "Mom, can I talk to you about something."

"Of course."

He pulled her aside into the master bedroom where she'd be staying with his father. He'd already moved his stuff to the smaller room. She sat down on the trunk at the foot of the bed. He paced back and forth a few times, running his fingers through his hair when he finally came to a stop.

"What is it, hon?" She stood and placed her hand on his shoulder.

He took a deep breath. "I think I want to ask Holly to marry me."

"Holly? Who is Holly?" She sat back down.

"My landlady. The woman who rented me this place. She lives next door."

"Oh. Okay."

"I haven't known her long, but I know she's the one."

"That's wonderful, Noel." His mother wrapped her arms around him.

He pulled back, so he could see her face. "You don't think it's too soon?"

"If you know, you know."

"So, I have your blessing?"

"Of course. I'd like to meet her though."

"I'm going to ask her to come over now, but I wanted to talk to you first, so you would know that she isn't simply a neighbor."

"I can't wait to meet this lovely young lady who has captured my son's heart."

"Thanks, Mom." He kissed her cheek and went to talk to his father.

Within thirty minutes, he'd had the talk with everyone in his family. His older sister, Sheila, was skeptical, but the rest of his family seemed genuinely happy for him.

Noel knocked on the door to Holly's kitchen and waited for her to answer it.

"Since when do you wait for me to answer the door?"

Toby jumped up on him, and Noel scratched behind his ears.

"I don't know why I didn't let myself in. I was hoping you would agree to come over. Meet my crazy family."

"Sure. I have to finish cleaning up this mess

first. Come on in."

He leaned on the kitchen counter, too wound up to sit. "Anything new?"

"Doctor called with biopsy results."

"And?"

"He was right."

"That disorder he was talking about?"

"Ehlers-Danlos Syndrome. Classical Type."

"It has more than one type?"

"Quite a few apparently. I spent hours looking it up last night."

"I'll bet."

"It's a connective tissue disease that affects the collagen. The symptoms fit. I thought some of them were normal for everyone. Some of the types can't be diagnosed by biopsy, so I guess I lucked out that this one can."

"It's not luck."

"I guess not."

"What are the symptoms?"

"Some are seemingly harmless, like stretchy skin and flexibility. Others aren't so minor, like organ prolapses, gastrointestinal issues, frequent dislocations, and severe cervical problems."

"That sounds frightening." He took her hands in his.

She stared at the counter. "It ought to sufficiently scare off anyone dumb enough to get involved with me. I suppose it's a good thing I didn't plan on marrying again."

"Why wouldn't you marry?" He reached out and tilted her chin up. Looked into her liquid-brown eyes. "You will make some man an exceptional wife. A few trips to the hospital for dislocations and various ailments won't change that. If you spent the rest of your days in a wheelchair, you would still bring yourself to a relationship. Your fun, feisty, fabulous self. I can't think of anything more a man could want."

"Authors aren't supposed to use that many adjectives."

"That's what you got out of that sentence?" He pulled her into his arms. His thoughts betrayed him. He'd meant what he said, but it would be a huge step asking a woman to marry him when he knew going in the serious health concerns she faced. He held her, running circles on her back with his finger for a long while, before stroking her hair and lifting her face, so that he could kiss her.

"Noel, aren't you leaving in a few short days?" Holly pulled away.

"Shh." He didn't tell her he'd planned to bring her with him. He didn't ask her to be his girl. He simply pulled her back into his arms. Kissed her again, hoping she'd feel what he couldn't vocalize. Hoping she would see that she meant everything to him and that he didn't want to leave her behind.

Holly pulled away again.

"I'm going to go freshen up. I'll be over in a few minutes, if you still want me to come over?"

"Of course, I want you to come." She left the room and he remained rooted in place. Toby kissed his hand. It was another man's dog, but it sensed his angst. He reached into his pocket and felt the ring. He let out a deep sigh and dragged himself next door.

Knocking on the door of her childhood home felt strange. Holly balanced cupcakes in one hand while knocking with the other. There was no doorbell for the back door, and she didn't feel like walking around to the front. It took a few minutes, but a beautiful woman with strawberry-blonde hair that reached her waist finally answered. "You must be Holly. Come on in."

"Hi. One of Noel's sisters?"

"Yes. I'm Stephanie. I'll take you in to meet the rest of the gang. Don't let them overwhelm you. They can be a little rambunctious."

"Oh, Holly, good you're here." Noel hurried to her side. "I want you to meet my family. It looks like you already met Stephanie. He pointed to each sibling as he introduced them. My brother Nathan will be here later, he's driving in this afternoon. He introduced, Samantha, Sheila, Sonya, Stacy, and Sally, before moving on to his parents, Jonathan and Marny.

"How come the boys names don't start with

an 's' like the girls?" Holly asked.

"We thought it would be neat to give the boys names that started with an 'n' and the girls' names that started with an 's.' We're just weird like that. Sometimes they'd like to kill us for it." Marny laughed good-naturedly.

Jonathan asked, "Have you lived in the area long, Holly?"

"I grew up in this house."

"And now you live next door?"

"Yes, my husband and I built the house next door on my parents' property."

"And what happened to your husband?" Jonathan asked.

Holly's face warmed. She wasn't used to be questioned. She felt like a teenager. Noel came to her rescue. "Dad, chill. I'll fill you in later."

The youngest sister, Sally, grabbed Holly's arm. "Come on. Let's put our coats on and go out and make a snowman." She was totally on board with that idea if it took her out of the spotlight. She had trouble keeping up with Sally, who moved faster than her sore hip would allow. Before she knew what was happening, they had a five-foot=tall snowman, with black licorice eyes and a red licorice mouth. They didn't have a carrot, so they didn't know what to use for a nose. Sally found a pinecone. They both laughed. The pinecone wasn't going to cut it for a nose. Noel came out with a candy cane and stuck it into the snow, so the round end protruded out, forming a nose. She giggled at his ingenuity. Sally grabbed her by the arm and pulled her behind the SUV. The first snowball hit Noel between the shoulders. "You ladies better watch it. Payback time." He disappeared into the house and came back with Neil. Before long, all the siblings had joined in and there was snow flying everywhere. After one particularly good shot to the chest, Noel rushed Holly, pushing her into a snowbank. He snatched a kiss while his siblings were preoccupied slamming each other with snowballs. Holly felt a tremor go through her at his nearness.

"You're cold." Noel mistook her emotion for chills and helped her up out of the snow and into her house. She didn't correct him. Why not sneak a few moments alone with the man she'd come to love before he left? He took her hand and walked with her until they were inside. When he released her, the separation was painful. She moved close to him and put her head on his coat-clad chest.

"Hey. Are you okay?" He held her chin and caressed her cheek with his thumb.

She forced herself to take a step back, putting some distance between them. "I'm fine. I'll go put some dry clothes on. You can stick your coat in the dryer if you want."

"It'll dry on its own. I'll wait here for you."

"You should probably get back to your family."

"Nathan and Jenna just pulled up. They're busy saying their hellos. We can greet him when you're ready." Holly sighed inwardly. So much for a few minutes alone with Noel.

Noel sat by the fireplace waiting for Holly to come downstairs. He stared down at the package in his trembling hands. Looking up at the ceiling, he shot a prayer upward asking the Lord for His blessing. Holly was determined to remain alone for the rest of her life. She'd made that abundantly clear. Was there room in her life for him? Would she even consider his proposal? In the brief time he'd known her, she'd become a vital part of his life. Watching her Friday night as she handled all the details of the pageant with poise and grace, it hit him that she was the one. And today, seeing her with his family, he was further convinced. There was no other woman for him. He couldn't imagine going home and leaving her behind. What if that was what she wanted? Could he abide by her wishes and walk out of her life, never to return? It didn't seem possible, but if it was what she wanted, he'd force himself to leave. It wouldn't be easy. It would break his heart, but he would go.

He watched as she descended the stairs. There were no words to adequately convey his emotions. She'd dressed elegantly in a simple black dress that flared out at her hips. The woman was breathtaking. He wanted nothing more than to make this woman his wife. "Are you ready to head to church?" she asked.

"Not yet." His voice cracked.

"We'll be late if we don't leave soon."

"I know." He reached for her, ready to pose the question. At that moment her telephone rang, and she went to answer it. When she hung up, she slipped her coat on and moved to the door. He felt little choice but to follow. His family saw them come out the door and looked at him expectantly. He shook his head. They probably thought she'd said no. He'd have to explain later.

The candlelight service was beautiful. He enjoyed the sermon and felt caught up in his feelings about all that his Savior had done for him. Why would He leave His heavenly throne to come down here? It baffled him that God showed him such an undeserved love. Even if Holly said no tonight, he'd be complete, knowing Jesus was all he needed. But, man, he really hoped she'd say yes. What was it the Bible said in Proverbs? The words came to him silently. "Whoso findeth a wife findeth a good thing, and obtaineth favour of the LORD." It seemed to be an answer directly from God. The verse was a familiar one, but the words coming to him when he asked for them could be nothing less than an answer from the Almighty.

After service, Holly mingled with her friends and neighbors, and he caught up with his parents to let them know that he hadn't been able to ask her yet. He saw his brother, Nathan, corner Holly and hurried over to rescue her.

"You should know that he's not the handsome brother. That would be me," Nathan said.

"The handsome, married brother," Noel interjected when he walked up.

"Ah. There you are. I was spending some time getting to know your future bride."

"His what?" Holly sputtered.

Noel shot him a look that would shrivel a lesser man. Nathan simply shrugged and sauntered away.

"Ignore him. Are you almost ready?"

"Sure. I just need to touch base with Casey for a second."

"Okay. I'll wait by the doors."

Chapter 7

Back at Holly's place, Noel lit a fire and paced the floor while Holly prepared cocoa. He tried to come up with the perfect way to pop the question. A best-selling author should be able to craft words for a marriage proposal. Right?

The scent of lilacs drew his attention as she stepped into the room. She had topped the mugs of white chocolate cocoa with peppermint candy canes and baby marshmallows.

"That looks good," he said.

"Shall we sit by the fire and enjoy it?" she asked.

"Definitely."

She set the mugs on the table and crossed the room to the Christmas tree. She had packages piled up on a table beside it. After removing one from the pile, she went and sat beside him. "I got this for you."

He gently removed the paper and opened the

box. It was a dark blue Christmas tie featuring the nativity scene. Lying on top of it was a gold tie-clip shaped like a quill pen. "I love it. I have one for you too." He handed her the first box, a large one that he'd stashed by the tree earlier.

She tore the paper away and pulled out the tiered cupcake case. "This is perfect. I desperately needed one of these."

"I'm glad you like it." He sat forward on his chair and clasped his hands in front of him. "Now, Holly, do you promise I have your full attention for a few minutes."

"Sure. Why what's up?" She twisted her bracelet around and around her wrist, revealing her nervousness.

He got down on one knee in front of the fireplace and pulled the wrapped box from his pocket. He waited for her to open it. Her eyes widened when she saw the ring. He reached over and removed the ring from the box. Holding it up to the fire he watched the diamonds reflect its light. Then he focused in on her eyes. They were shiny with unshed tears. "Will you marry me, Holly Ewing?"

"Are you serious?" She shook her head. The dam released and her tears flowed freely.

"Is that a no?"

"No. It's not a no. I can't imagine continuing my life without you. Yes, I'll marry you. I thought… I thought… well, I thought you were going to tell me that you were leaving and that it was over between us."

"How could you possibly think that? I've never given you any reason to doubt me, have I?"

"No. I suppose not. I knew your three-month lease was almost over, so I figured you'd be in a hurry to leave."

"I won't be going anywhere without you. If you want to stay, we'll stay. If you want to come back to Gladwyne, then we'll live there. If you want to move to Hawaii, Puerto Rico, or London, I'll take you there. I don't care where we live as long as we're together."

"I want to be wherever you are."

"That's all I needed to hear." He put the ring on her finger and scooped her up into his arms.

Sitting down on the sofa with her in his arms, he kissed her tenderly. It was a long time before they came up for air.

The smell of baked goods greeted him as Holly opened the door for him. He wiped flour off her cheek. And before he knew what he was doing, he pulled her close and kissed her. She yielded to his kiss, and he had to force himself to break the connection. He held her another long moment after ending the kiss. Placing a soft kiss on the top of her head, he released her.

"Something smells good in here."

"I've been baking since four."

"As usual."

"Want some pumpkin muffins? Coffee?"

"I'd love both. Thanks." He sat at kitchen table and watched as she scurried around the room. This is what Christmas should be like. Spent watching the woman he loved bustle about her kitchen with a smile on her face. What was she smiling about anyway? Holly looked like a mouse who outsmarted the cat. He hoped it was happiness over their pending nuptials. She handed him a cup of coffee and he savored the warmth of the cup in his hands.

"Aren't you supposed to be next door entertaining your family?" Holly sat down across from him at the table. She took a long sip of her coffee.

"My family is not awake. And if they were, they'd understand my wanting to spend Christmas morning with my fiancé."

Coffee came out of her nose as she laughed. She dabbed it with a napkin and looked at him incredulously. "You've got to be kidding? I would not understand if my family member wanted to spend Christmas with someone they'd met only months earlier instead of me."

"Do you have any family coming to town?"

"No."

"I'm sorry."

"It's what happens to only children, right?"

"Not necessarily, some have aunts, uncles, and cousins."

"I have an aunt and an uncle. One on each side. They have kids, so I have cousins, but I've only met them a couple of times in my life."

"Have you thought about reaching out?"

"Sometimes, but they're busy with their own lives. Why would I burden them?"

"Did it ever occur to you that it might be a joy for them to have you in their lives?"

Her laughter filled the room again. "No. I'm not full of myself."

"I think it's a joy to know you."

"You're insane."

"So, I've been told." He held his cup tightly to keep his hands still. "Please come over to-night."

"For what? Your family is there. You don't need me hanging around."

"Yes, I do. Please join us for Christmas dinner."

"But I have a ham to cook and was going to watch *It's a Wonderful Life*."

"It's settled then, you'll come over." He

smiled.

She nodded. "Fine. Yes, I'll come over, but I barely know your family. It will be awkward crashing your family dinner."

"I understand why you would think that, but you're wrong. You're part of the family now. They will love you like a daughter and a sister. Wait and see. If you come by around three, Samantha will be in the kitchen. She'll make sure you feel comfortable and welcome. Then I'll throw you back in with the pack of wild dogs."

"Don't you mean 'throw me to the wolves?'"

"Nope. I like it my way better."

Holly let herself into Noel's house. Samantha and Nathan's wife, Jenna, were in the kitchen cooking. Samantha handed Holly a spatula. An hour and several side dishes later, she finally made her way as far as the archway between the living and dining rooms.

Noel's family was scattered about. Several of them were seated on the floor. His mother smiled sweetly and pointed toward the mistletoe hanging above Holly. "Noel, your girl is under the mistletoe."

"I don't remember hanging any mistletoe."

"I added it," Noel grinned.

He didn't waste any time taking advantage of the situation. He kissed her thoroughly and she felt her insides turn to jelly. Life with this man was not going to be dull. Why had she thought she should remain alone for the remainder of her days? Nothing could be better than falling in love with this warm, sensitive man. The fact that he happened to provide her with an insta-family was a bonus. She loved the idea of having so many brothers and sisters.

"I'm going to throw cold water on you two if you don't break it up," Nathan said.

"Seriously! Maybe you should schedule the wedding for tonight," Sally said.

There was laughter all around.

Life with the Ryan family would be lively indeed.

www.ingramcontent.com/pod-product-compliance
Lightning Source LLC
Chambersburg PA
CBHW051957170626
46808CB00007B/2663